SUPER TURBO

AND THE FIRE-BREATHING DRAGON

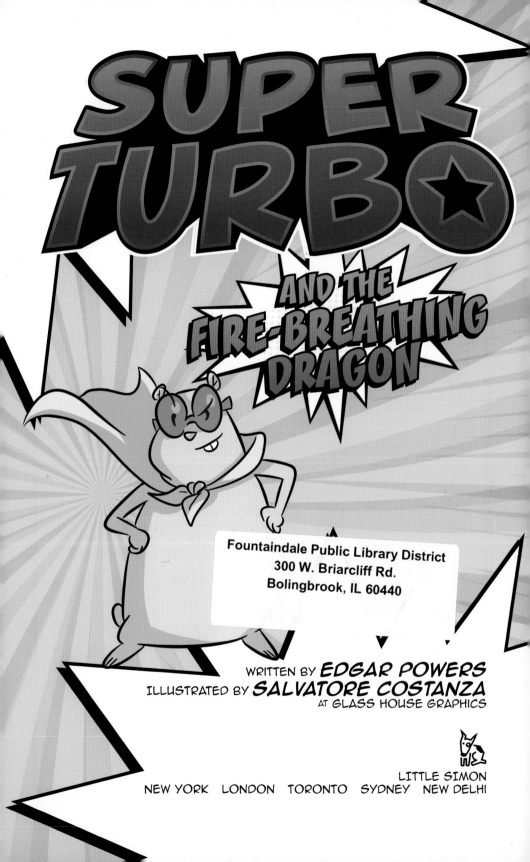

WRITTEN BY **EDGAR POWERS**
ILLUSTRATED BY **SALVATORE COSTANZA**
AT GLASS HOUSE GRAPHICS

LITTLE SIMON
NEW YORK LONDON TORONTO SYDNEY NEW DELHI

LITTLE SIMON
AN IMPRINT OF SIMON & SCHUSTER CHILDREN'S PUBLISHING DIVISION
1230 AVENUE OF THE AMERICAS, NEW YORK, NEW YORK 10020
FIRST LITTLE SIMON EDITION SEPTEMBER 2021 * COPYRIGHT © 2021 BY SIMON & SCHUSTER, INC. ALL RIGHTS RESERVED, INCLUDING THE RIGHT OF REPRODUCTION IN WHOLE OR IN PART IN ANY FORM. LITTLE SIMON IS A REGISTERED TRADEMARK OF SIMON & SCHUSTER, INC., AND ASSOCIATED COLOPHON IS A TRADEMARK OF SIMON & SCHUSTER, INC. FOR INFORMATION ABOUT SPECIAL DISCOUNTS FOR BULK PURCHASES, PLEASE CONTACT SIMON & SCHUSTER SPECIAL SALES AT 1-866-506-1949 OR BUSINESS@SIMONANDSCHUSTER.COM. THE SIMON & SCHUSTER SPEAKERS BUREAU CAN BRING AUTHORS TO YOUR LIVE EVENT. FOR MORE INFORMATION OR TO BOOK AN EVENT CONTACT THE SIMON & SCHUSTER SPEAKERS BUREAU AT 1-866-248-3049 OR VISIT OUR WEBSITE AT WWW.SIMONSPEAKERS.COM. DESIGNED BY NICHOLAS SCIACCA * ART SERVICES BY GLASS HOUSE GRAPHICS * ART AND COLOR BY SALVATORE COSTANZA * LETTERING BY GIOVANNI SPATARO/GRAFIMATED CARTOON * SUPERVISION BY SALVATORE DI MARCO/GRAFIMATED CARTOON * MANUFACTURED IN CHINA 0621 SCP * 2 4 6 8 10 9 7 5 3 1 * LIBRARY OF CONGRESS CATALOGING-IN-PUBLICATION DATA NAMES: POWERS, EDGAR J., AUTHOR. | GLASS HOUSE GRAPHICS, ILLUSTRATOR. TITLE: SUPER TURBO AND THE FIRE-BREATHING DRAGON / BY EDGAR J. POWERS ; ILLUSTRATED BY GLASS HOUSE GRAPHICS. DESCRIPTION: FIRST LITTLE SIMON EDITION. | NEW YORK : LITTLE SIMON, 2021. | SERIES: SUPER TURBO, THE GRAPHIC NOVEL ; BOOK 5 | AUDIENCE: AGES 5-9 | AUDIENCE: GRADES K-4 | SUMMARY: SUPER TURBO AND THE SUPERPETS AT SUNNYVIEW ELEMENTARY TRY TO GET RID OF THE FIRE-BREATHING DRAGON IN THE SCIENCE LAB BEFORE IT DOES SERIOUS DAMAGE. IDENTIFIERS: LCCN 2020049522 (PRINT) | LCCN 2020049523 (EBOOK) | ISBN 9781534485372 (PAPERBACK) | ISBN 9781534485389 (HARDCOVER) | ISBN 9781534485396 (EBOOK) SUBJECTS: LCSH: GRAPHIC NOVELS. | CYAC: GRAPHIC NOVELS. | SUPERHEROES—FICTION. | HAMSTERS—FICTION. | DRAGONS—FICTION. | ELEMENTARY SCHOOLS—FICTION. | SCHOOLS—FICTION. CLASSIFICATION: LCC PZ7.7.P7 SF 2021 (PRINT) | LCC PZ7.7.P7 (EBOOK) | DDC 741.5/973—DC23 LC RECORD AVAILABLE AT HTTPS://LCCN.LOC.GOV/2020049522 LC EBOOK RECORD AVAILABLE AT HTTPS://LCCN.LOC.GOV/2020049523

CONTENTS

BUT MORE ON THAT SOON!

7

THIS IS CLASSROOM C, ONE OF THE MANY CLASSROOMS INSIDE SUNNYVIEW ELEMENTARY.

DO YOU KNOW *WHO* LIVES HERE?

OF *COURSE* YOU DO! TURBO LIVES HERE! HE'S THE OFFICIAL CLASSROOM PET OF CLASSROOM C.

TURBO!
Official Classroom Pet
CLASSROOM C

HE'S USUALLY MORE CHEERFUL THAN THIS. WHAT'S *WRONG,* TURBO?

SIGH!

IT SEEMS LIKE TURBO ISN'T IN THE *MOOD* TO TALK TODAY. SO AS I WAS SAYING—

I WAS JUST ABOUT TO TELL YOU WHAT'S *WRONG!*

WHOOPS, SORRY, TURBO. THE FLOOR IS YOURS.

UNTIL YESTERDAY, MY FRIEND *NELL* WAS LIVING IN CLASSROOM C WITH ME. I MISS HER!

LAST NIGHT THEY *MOVED* NELL TO HER NEW AQUARIUM IN THE HALLWAY.

OF COURSE, IT WON'T BE LONG UNTIL I SEE HER AGAIN. AFTER ALL, WE HAVE *ANOTHER SUPERPET*—

WAIT, TURBO! WE HAVEN'T TOLD THEM ABOUT THAT YET!

UM, I THINK THEY ALREADY *KNOW* ABOUT THAT.

BUT GO AHEAD...

TURBO WILL SEE NELL AGAIN SOON BECAUSE THEY ARE BOTH *MEMBERS* OF...

...THE SUPERPET SUPERHERO LEAGUE!

WHICH MEANS TURBO IS *NO ORDINARY* HAMSTER. (THIS IS THE *SECRET* I MENTIONED EARLIER.)

HE'S *SUPER TURBO!*

AND NELL IS...*FANTASTIC FISH!*

LEO IS REALLY THE *GREAT GECKO!*

FRANK IS *BOSS BUNNY.*

ANGELINA IS *WONDER PIG.*

CLEVER IS THE *GREEN WINGER.*

AND LAST BUT NOT LEAST, WARREN IS *PROFESSOR TURTLE.*

PROFESSOR TURTLE IS THE *SLOWEST,* THOUGH, BECAUSE, WELL... HE'S A TURTLE.

THE OTHER SUPERPETS AND I **PROTECT** THE SCHOOL FROM THE **EVIL** THAT IS ALL AROUND US.

AND BELIEVE ME, THERE IS EVIL **EVERYWHERE** AT THIS SCHOOL!

PROBABLY THE BIGGEST VILLAIN HERE IS **WHISKERFACE.**

HE'S A **MOUSE** WHO THINKS HE'S A **RAT.** THAT'S A LONG STORY, BUT HE'S EVIL.

HE WANTS TO TAKE OVER THE SCHOOL, AND THE **WORLD.**

BUT HE WON'T SUCCEED AS LONG AS THE SUPERPETS ARE HERE TO **STOP** HIM!

TIME TO GET THIS PLACE READY.

WE NEED LIGHTS...

...AND I'LL JUST *TIDY* UP A BIT.

ALL SET! NOW WE WAIT FOR THE OTHER SUPERPETS TO ARRIVE!

HEY, TURBO! WHAT'S SHAKING?

WONDER PIG WAS THE *FIRST* TO ARRIVE.

THE SUPERPETS TRAVELED AROUND THE SCHOOL THROUGH THE *VENT SYSTEM.* PRETTY CLEVER, RIGHT?

BEFORE LONG, THE OTHER SUPERPETS *ARRIVED.*

SO THE SUPERPETS *WAITED*...

...AND *WAITED*.

UNTIL FINALLY...

I THINK NEXT TIME PROFESSOR TURTLE NEEDS TO GET A *HEAD START*.

OKAY, LET'S BEGIN!

THE FIRST ORDER OF BUSINESS IS... HAPPY BIRTHDAY, ANGELINA!

HAPPY BIRTHDAY, ANGELINA!

THANKS!

AFTER THE MEETING IS OVER, WE'LL HEAD TO THE CAFETERIA FOR A SPECIAL *TREAT!*

SO, WHO HAS SOMETHING TO *REPORT?*

I DO!

FIVE KINDS OF CORAL? SOUNDS *FANCY!*

AND...A... *TOP...SECRET...* CAVE? WOW!

I CAN'T WAIT TO SEE YOUR NEW AQUARIUM! IT SOUNDS *AMAZING!*

I'M SUPER HAPPY FOR YOU!

I *MISS* HAVING YOU HERE IN CLASSROOM C, BUT YOUR NEW AQUARIUM REALLY DOES SOUND AWESOME.

I HAVE SOMETHING TO *REPORT!*

I PERFECTED A NEW *TRICK!* IT'S THE NINE-FLIP TWIST-AND-WHIRL!

LET'S *SEE* IT!

OKAY, HERE GOES...

OKAY, WHO'S NEXT?

I... HAVE...SOME... NEWS.

AS YOU CAN IMAGINE, IT TOOK PROFESSOR TURTLE *A WHILE* TO SHARE HIS NEWS.

THEY USED ALL THEIR BEST LISTENING SKILLS TO WAIT PATIENTLY.

BUT THE ANNOUNCEMENT WAS WORTH WAITING FOR, BECAUSE IT WAS A *BIG* ONE!

DR. GARFIELD ANNOUNCED THAT THERE WILL BE A *SURPRISE* WAITING IN THE SCIENCE CLASSROOM TOMORROW?

MAYBE NELL'S AQUARIUM IS BEING *MOVED* INTO CLASSROOM C!

MAYBE THEY'RE GETTING A BUNCH OF *NEW BOOKS* IN MY CLASSROOM!

LET'S HEAD OVER TO THE CAFETERIA.

33

BEFORE LONG, THE SUPERPETS REACHED THE *CAFETERIA.*

AND NOW IT'S TIME FOR YOUR BIRTHDAY *SURPRISE,* ANGELINA.

HE WAS STILL THINKING ABOUT THE *SURPRISE.*

BY THE TIME THE STUDENTS ARRIVED, TURBO WAS STILL THINKING ABOUT THE *SURPRISE.*

WHILE THE STUDENTS TOOK A MATH QUIZ, TURBO THOUGHT ABOUT THE *SURPRISE.*

TURBO THOUGHT ABOUT THE *SURPRISE* DURING MS. BEASLEY'S GEOGRAPHY LESSON.

TURBO STOPPED THINKING ABOUT THE *SURPRISE* FOR A LITTLE WHILE DURING RECESS.

BUT HE DECIDED THAT PROBABLY WASN'T A GREAT IDEA. HE WOULD JUST HAVE TO *WAIT* UNTIL THE END OF THE DAY.

FINALLY IT WAS TIME!

RING-A-DING-DING!

THE SCHOOL DAY WAS *OVER!*

THE CLASSROOM WAS EMPTY.

I'VE GOT TO GO CHECK ON *WARREN!*

BUT THEN TURBO HEARD THE SUPERPET DISTRESS *SIGNAL!*

BANG! BANG! BANG!

THAT SOUNDS LIKE A *BEAKER!*

ALL THE SUPERPETS HAD SPECIAL *ITEMS* THEY USED TO MAKE NOISE IN THE VENTS FOR DISTRESS SIGNALS.

TURBO KNEW THAT *PROFESSOR TURTLE'S* ITEM WAS A BEAKER.

GOTTA GO! PROFESSOR TURTLE NEEDS US!

SUPER TURBO RACED THROUGH THE VENT, TOWARD THE SCIENCE LAB. UNTIL...

OOF!

ARE YOU OKAY, TURBO?

I'M FINE. SORRY FOR *CRASHING* INTO YOU!

I JUST REALLY WANT TO GO SEE PROFESSOR TURTLE.

ME TOO!

I'VE HAD A *BAD* FEELING ABOUT THIS *SURPRISE* ALL DAY.

ME *TOO!*

THEY WERE SOON JOINED BY THE OTHER SUPERPETS. EVERYONE WAS RUSHING TO SEE WHY PROFESSOR TURTLE HAD USED THE DISTRESS SIGNAL!

PROFESSOR TURTLE?

WE'RE HERE!

I'LL FLY UP AND SEE WHAT'S *INSIDE* THE TANK!

WHAT'S INSIDE?

I CAN'T SEE ANYTHING! IT'S LIKE A *JUNGLE* IN THERE!

CAN SOMEONE ELSE COME UP?

UGH!

ALMOST THERE!

PHEW! MADE IT!

I'LL GO TAKE A CLOSER LOOK INSIDE.

CHAPTER 4

HERE'S THE *PLAN!*

THE SUPERPETS SPRANG INTO ACTION.

THEY *LIFTED.*

THEY *HEAVED.*

THEY PULLED.

THEY PUSHED.

AND EVENTUALLY THEY *ALL MADE IT!*

NOW... WHAT?

NOW WE ALL *LOOK INSIDE!*

ON THE COUNT OF THREE!

ONE...

TWO...

THREE!

THE SUPERPETS **WAITED.**

AND **WAITED.**

AND **WAITED** SOME MORE.

UNTIL FINALLY...

SOMETHING IS **MOVING** IN THERE!

...THE *CREATURE* EMERGED!

LET'S GO!

THE SUPERPETS **RAN!**

EVEN PROFESSOR TURTLE **HUSTLED!**

THEY MADE THEIR WAY DOWN TO THE FLOOR, TO **SAFETY!**

THEN THEY PAUSED FOR A MOMENT TO CATCH THEIR BREATH.

DID...YOU...GUYS...SEE...HOW...*FAST*...I...MOVED?

DOES ANYONE KNOW WHAT THAT *THING* IS?

CHAPTER 5

AFTER ANGELINA'S ANNOUNCEMENT, THE SUPERPETS *RACED* BACK TO THE SAFETY OF CLASSROOM C.

THE SUPERPETS NEEDED A *PLAN!*

BUT FIRST THEY ALL NEEDED TO CATCH THEIR BREATH AGAIN.

WE NEED A *PLAN!* LET'S ALL THINK REALLY HARD!

I'VE GOT IT!

LEO, SINCE YOU LOOK LIKE A *TINY* VERSION OF A DRAGON, MAYBE YOU CAN GO PRETEND TO BE A FIRE-BREATHING *DRAGON* YOURSELF!

WHAT GOOD WOULD THAT DO? WE NEED TO GET THE DRAGON OUT OF OUR SCHOOL.

OH YEAH. I DIDN'T FIGURE *THAT PART* OUT YET.

WE COULD **KNOCK** THE DRAGON'S TERRARIUM OFF THE DESK!

WE DON'T WANT TO **HURT** THE DRAGON!

THE TRUTH WAS, SUPER TURBO HAD AN *IDEA* TOO.

BUT HIS PLAN WAS RISKY. *VERY RISKY.*

THIS PLAN OF SUPER TURBO'S? IT INVOLVED *WHISKERFACE!*

I HAVE AN IDEA...

LET'S HEAR IT!

WELL, YOU KNOW HOW WHISKERFACE IS ALWAYS TRYING TO GET RID OF US?

RIGHT, BUT HIS PLANS NEVER WORK BECAUSE WE ALWAYS *STOP* HIM!

EXACTLY! BUT IF WE WORK *WITH HIM*...THEN MAYBE...

...WE CAN GET RID OF THE FIRE-BREATHING DRAGON TOGETHER!

BUT THE *MORE* THEY CONSIDERED IT...

...THE *MORE* THEY REALIZED IT JUST MIGHT WORK!

YOU KNOW WHAT, TURBO? YOUR PLAN IS *WILD*, BUT IT MIGHT BE *GENIUS!*

WHO ELSE IS *IN?*

WHISKERFACE!

SPECIFICALLY, THEY KNEW HE LIVED IN THE WALL IN THE *PANTRY*. AND THAT'S WHERE HE WAS.

EH?

RAT PACK! WHO DARES TO DISTURB MY BEAUTY REST?

SIR, IT'S THE... SUPERPETS!

THE SUPER*PESTS?* TAKE ME TO THEM!

TURBO EXPLAINED THE SITUATION TO WHISKERFACE, WHO SAID...

NOW WHAT?

TO THE SCIENCE LAB!

OUR ENEMY IS UP THERE!

WAIT!

DO YOU *SMELL* THAT?

YOU CAN SMELL THAT? I HAD *TACO* SCRAPS FROM THE GARBAGE FOR LUNCH—DON'T *JUDGE* ME.

NO, THAT'S NOT WHAT I MEAN. IT *SMELLS* LIKE...

IT SMELLS LIKE...

...FIRE!

THE SUPERPETS KNEW JUST WHAT TO DO!

THE FIRE IS OUT!

BUT HOW DID IT *START?*

IT HAD BEEN A LONG NIGHT. AND TURBO WAS *EXHAUSTED.*

AND SO WERE ALL THE OTHER SUPERPETS. SINCE THEY HAD NOWHERE TO BE UNTIL AFTER SCHOOL, MOST OF THEM SPENT THE DAY *SLEEPING.*

BUT NOT ALL THE SUPERPETS.

NO PAIN, NO GAIN.

WARREN, HOWEVER, WAS CATCHING UP ON HIS *SLEEP.*

WHICH WAS WHY HE MISSED IT WHEN DR. GARFIELD SAID *THIS...*

DID YOU **HEAR** THAT? THE FIRE WAS NOT CAUSED BY THE FIRE-BREATHING DRAGON!

AS THE END OF THE SCHOOL DAY NEARED, THE PETS ALL BEGAN TO GET READY FOR THEIR **MEETING** WITH WHISKERFACE.

FINALLY IT WAS **TIME!**

RIIIIIING!

THE CROWD OF RAT PACKERS PARTED AS THE SUPERPETS MADE THEIR WAY INTO THE PANTRY.

LET'S *HEAR* IT, THEN.

HEAR WHAT?

UM, YOUR *PLAN?* YOU DO HAVE ONE, RIGHT?

I HAVE A PLAN! BUT I ALSO HAVE A *PREPARED SPEECH* READY, SO BE QUIET AND *LISTEN!*

REMEMBER, WE TOLD YOU WE DON'T WANT ANY HARM DONE TO THE FIRE-BREATHING DRAGON!

WE JUST WANT IT OUT OF THE SCHOOL.

SO NOTHING DANGEROUS!

WE ARE SERIOUS! WE CAN'T HURT—

STEP 1: You open the science lab door for me.

ME

STEP 2: My Rat Pack forms a pyramid. I'll be on top, of course.

← ME, AGAIN

STEP 3: You pampered pets remove the lid of the terrarium.

STEP 4: I use a feather to tickle the fire-breathing dragon.

STEP 5: While it's laughing, we tie it up.

STEP 6: We lift the dragon out of the terrarium and toss it out the window.

THAT'S ACTUALLY **NOT** A **BAD** PLAN.

I AGREE. THERE ARE BUSHES OUTSIDE THE WINDOW, SO WE WOULDN'T **HURT** THE DRAGON WHEN WE TOSS IT OUT THE WINDOW.

LET'S DO THIS!

NOW OPEN THE LID!

OKAY, NOW IT'S *YOUR* TURN!

HA HA HA!

YOU *FELL* FOR IT!

I'M...

...RIGHT...

...HERE!

THE DRAGON
TURNED RED TO
BREATHE FIRE!

CHAPTER 9

SUPER TURBO AND THE OTHER SUPERPETS FACED DOWN THE *FIRE-BREATHING DRAGON*, SURE THAT THEY WERE ABOUT TO BE *EXTINGUISHED*.

UNTIL SUPER TURBO *NOTICED* SOMETHING.

ARE YOU... *CRYING?*

YES. I KNOW YOU GUYS WANT TO *GET RID* OF ME. I'M JUST NOT SURE *WHY.*

I'VE BEEN TRYING TO MIND MY OWN BUSINESS...BUT IT SEEMS I SHOULD JUST GO.

I *LOVE* IT HERE!

I LOVE BEING A CLASSROOM *PET!*

BUT LIKE I SAID, I GUESS IT'S BEST FOR ME TO JUST *LEAVE.*

BUT...BUT... AREN'T YOU A FIRE-BREATHING DRAGON?

A KA-*WHAT?*

A CHAMELEON!

WHAT DOES THAT MEAN? I'VE NEVER MET A—A CHAMELEON!

I'M A SPECIAL KIND OF *LIZARD.* I CAN CHANGE COLOR...BUT I DEFINITELY *CANNOT* BREATHE FIRE!

WE'RE SO *SORRY!* WE WERE JUST TRYING TO PROTECT OUR SCHOOL.

BECAUSE WE THOUGHT...YOU WANTED TO SET *FIRE* TO IT.

THAT'S OKAY... I'M JUST REALLY GLAD YOU DON'T ACTUALLY WANT TO *GET RID* OF ME!

DEFINITELY NOT!

WHISKERFACE CLAIMS HE'S A *RAT*...BUT WE ALL KNOW HE'S A *MOUSE*.

HE SURE ACTS LIKE A RAT, THOUGH! HE'S *EVIL!*

HE'S THE REAL EVIL WE NEED TO PROTECT THE SCHOOL FROM!

WELL, I'M NOT A *SUPERPET*, BUT...

THE SCHOOL HAD BEEN SAVED YET AGAIN, THANKS TO THE *SUPERPET SUPERHERO LEAGUE...*

WONDER PIG FORGET ABOUT A MEETING IN THE CAFETERIA WITH *FOOD?*

THAT DOESN'T SOUND LIKE HER!

IT SURE DOESN'T. I—

BEFORE TURBO COULD FINISH HIS THOUGHT, *THIS* HAPPENED:

A BAG OF CHEEZIE DOODLES STARTED *MOVING* BY ITSELF!

CHEEZIE DOODLES